Bud's Space Adventure

Odette Ross

Puffin Baby

Tonight Bud can see the moon.

5

4

3

2

1

BLAST OFF!

Bud explores outer space.

He catches a star.

And rides on a comet.

But, oh no!
An alien steals Bud's rocket.

How will he return home?

A friendly Martian
lends Bud his space ship.

And Bud flies over the moon.

Around the planets.

And back home to bed.
Good night, Bud!